Wild, Imperfect & Messy

by

Xtina Marie

A HellBound Books LLC Publication
Copyright © 2021 by HellBound Books Publishing LLC
All Rights Reserved

Cover and art design by Luke Spooner

for
HellBound Books Publishing LLC

No part of this book may be reproduced, stored in a retrieval system, or transmitted by any means, electronic, mechanical, photocopying, recording or otherwise without written permission from the author
This book is a work of fiction. Names, characters, places and incidents are entirely fictitious or are used fictitiously and any resemblance to actual persons, living or dead, events or locales is purely coincidental.

www.hellboundbookspublishing.com

Printed in the United States of America

Acknowledgements

I always start by acknowledging the people who helped make this book a reality:

Thank you to Denise Jury, who proofreads and gives me pointers on how to make my writing even better. She's the one who sees most poems before anyone else and tells me that I don't suck!

Thank you to my amazing cover artist, Luke Spooner, whose work keeps getting more amazing.

Thank you to my wonderful future husband who works daily to free me from the demons of my past.

And last but definitely not least, thank you James Longmore, my friend and business partner, for all that you do!

"We are made of all those who have built and broken us."

—Atticus Poetry, Love Her Wild

Contents:

Xtina Marie

True love
is untidy
wild
imperfect
and messy

Xtina Marie

Your Creation

I'm your
canvas,
your
creation,
my creamy
skin
awaits
your
implement
of choice,
the anticipation
steals the
air
from my
lungs
as I
lie here
in want
in need
in submission

Autumn

remember autumn
and the
sweetness
of your lips
I'd forgotten

To North Carolina

On a mountain road
that leads
from Tennessee to
North Carolina,
I caught a glimpse
of this house
mostly hidden
from sight
in the brush,
gone so
quickly
if I'd have
blinked
I would have
missed it,
but there it was,
this lone house
in the middle
of nothing
with only
the white noise
of the traffic below
promising
to never reveal

the secrets
hidden in the
hurried glance
the road provided
16

I Seek

When the world
closes in,
gets too loud,
starts to blur
around me
I seek
the warmth,
the comfort,
the security
of your arms
to hold me

lingers

the sweet
taste
of a
goodbye
kiss
lingers
longingly

Not My Own

My will
not my own
I lay
vulnerable
my pleasure
yours
as you feast
on me
my moans
become screams
and drown out
the roaring of
my heart
my will
not my own

Old Ghosts

listening
to the
soft pelts
on the
windowpane
and wondering
if it's
raining
where
you are
and if
you're
wondering
the same

Van Halen

Van Halen
came on the radio—
not even
"our song"
but still I paused,
took a breath
at the
stabbing pain
shooting
through me
as I recalled
the last time
we spoke,
as I was flooded
with memories
and the deep
timbre
of your voice,
as I remembered
the harsh words
you spat at me
in place of a
proper goodbye
and now I know

why this could
never be
love

Devour

the dead
of the
night,
no sounds
but the house
settling,
or the soft
breathing
beside me,
it comes
for me,
with hands
outstretched
and reaching,
long talons
protruding
from skeletal
fingers,
the stink of
death and
decay
lingering,
and I pull
the comforter

higher,
wondering
how long
until I
allow
the nightmare
to devour me
whole

Endless Possibilities

I fall a little
in love
with the poets
I read
as I linger
over the words
carefully picked
out of *all* the words
and I wonder
is this a work of
fiction
or is this their truth
or perhaps
something in between?
did he sip coffee
while penning this poem,
does he even fancy coffee,
black? or cream and 2 sugars?
the possibilities are
endless
and I ponder
what he's like—
dark and brooding?
is that just a façade,

a persona he dons
when he grabs his pen
he'd look good with a
quill, don't you think?
I wonder if he has one
just for show, not a real one
but one on display
somewhere where he can
see it while he writes
does he anguish
over each line
or do they flow
like fine wine?
is he the cliched poet
with bouts of depression
sprinkled with alcoholism
as his comrades,
or is he the life of the party
bellowing with laughter
while he partakes of
novelty drugs that are
fashionable in certain circles
the possibilities are endless
and will I ever know?

Pulsing Amber

I've never once
been close to
halting
playtime with
crimson visions
playing about my
tongue
calling out
the safe word,
"Red"
pushing past
lips stretched
in pain
endorphins
racing through
a body
struggling to
focus on
the intensity
moments before
succumbing
to the space between
with shades of
pulsing amber

dancing

Too Girly

I've been ridiculed
for being
too girly
but I much prefer
the feel
of a cotton skirt
floating around
my thighs
to the rough
scratch
of blue jeans,
and I fancy
dusty rose pink
even though
that's not
the cool answer
to what's your
favorite color.
If my nails
aren't painted,
check my forehead—
I may be feverish
and please
don't ever ask me

to help you
work on the car,
but I'll happily
sit in the shade
and fan myself
while I watch
you sweat

Occasionally
the dark
whispers
and she
understood
the crazed
language

one key moment
a spark
a connection
can make
anything
last

Broken

when you're
broken
you don't know
you're broken
you don't feel
broken
you just feel
…nothing
at all
a void
emptiness
cold
nothingness
you can
scream
into the
abyss
and no one
but you
can hear the
echoes
bouncing back
surrounding
the pieces

the fragments
of the
broken
thing
you've
become

Swallow

Drowning
in oblivion
you shout
beautiful
nothings
and I
swallow

My Name

Nana left—
her mind
slipped
through
an open door,
back to
when
she was
twenty something—
outside the
window
an interesting
display,
discarded trinkets
she collected
but soon forgot
along with
my name

Vapid Words

We enjoy
and over-indulge
vapid words
rolling off tongues
that lap them up,
devour them
afraid they'll
disappear
before we're
fully satiated
and in lonely times
we regurgitate,
savoring their taste
all over again

The Mirror

I used to
have trouble
meeting my eyes
in the mirror
self confidence
gone
massacred
depleted
from years of
insults
slights
verbal humiliations
spoken only
with the intent
to hurt
and tear down
hurled carelessly
daily, hourly
by the person
claiming
unconditional
devotion

but now

daily, hourly

you make time
to build me up
with more than
words
with eyes
that follow me
when I leave
your warm bed
in the morning
no make-up
and hair a mess
or when I'm
hot and sweaty
in the kitchen
apron dirty
from whatever
dinner was
that night
and without
even realizing it
I am talking to
myself
having a whole
conversation
while brushing my teeth
staring intently
at my reflection
with a smile
on my lips

Honey and Bourbon

I carry
a piece of
you
with me
still,
a part
that lies
dormant
most of the
time,
a part
I try to
ignore
when I hear
a song
that used to
remind me
of you,
but I catch
myself
singing along
and wondering
what you're doing,
how you're doing
and if you
think of me at night—
our time,

when we'd
talk for
hours
and I'd
pretend to
pay attention
when really
all I focused on
was the deep
timbre
of your voice
and the way
every word
dripped honey
and bourbon
and I drank them
down like I
was moments
from death
and needed them
to sustain
my life
the empty life
I'd lived
before you

Burn

I go crazy
daily
with the
chaos
of our world
the hatred
being bred
spreading
faster
than the summer
wildfires
so unpredictable
uncontrollable
and so very
devastating
to all
living things
and deep down
under all
the differences
we're being
programmed
to notice—

we all

burn

the

same

Sometimes
it's nice
to know
they
still think
of us
even if
it's not
always
fondly

The Albatross

I once
compared
myself
to an
albatross
around
your neck
a burden
a hindrance
something
you begrudgingly
allowed
to monopolize
your time
your energy
and I felt
fortunate
lucky
blessed
to be
granted
space

in your
life
before tasting
how bitter
the pill
you were
force feeding me,
how suffocating
the embrace
strangling me,
and how
poisonous
the lips
kissing me

One More Taste

I'm pretty sure
it wasn't
an apple
that Eve
held out to
Adam
and damned
all of
creation
with just
one taste,
but the
succulent
heart shaped
nectarine;
its flavor
bursting
in your mouth,
the warm
juices
sliding
over your
tongue

to coat
your throat,
the sticky
heavenly
nectar
shining from
plump lips
and the
knowledge
that he'd
gladly
willingly
damn us
all over again
for just
one more
taste

Salt

Lick
the salt
from my
eyes
when the
stars begin
to run

Almost Painful

I was
deprived
for so long
the proper
affection
and love
that when
you first
reached for me
in the night
I recoiled
in discomfort,
the touch
almost painful
it was so
alien…
almost—
and now
when an hour
has passed
and I
haven't felt
the heat of

your fingers
on my
creamy flesh,
I yearn
ache
crave
for the contact,
and it's
almost painful;
the absence
of your warmth—
almost…

The Margaritas

Maybe
it was the
Margaritas
whispering
through my blood
or the moon
so big, and bright
and looking
a million
miles away,
or perhaps it was
the way
Ozzy sang
about roads
and the
haunting past
while we sped
through the darkness
on the country 2 lane
in your sportscar,
but all of the
world's problems
and all of my
daily inconveniences
skittered away
like the opossum
darting out at us

with no thought
to the dangers
he'd just avoided—

it might
have been
the Margaritas

Hollow

Why won't you
just die?
I remember
flinging
the words
at you
like I'd
hurled those
lawn darts
at the neighbor boy
when he wouldn't
stop laughing
that time I fell
and ripped
my jeans
right in the bum

snot and tears
plastered
to my
blotched face
as the nurse
told me
to leave the room
while she
prepared
your hand

for the IV you'd need
to replenish the fluids
depleted
on this latest
binge

but you didn't

die
I mean

And as I stare
at the hollow
eyes
in the pictures
I still have
of you
it's clear
you wish
you had

Escaping You

It's dark
late
must be at least
3am
and I have work
in the morning
and it'll be another
shift
I stumble in for
exhausted, yet relieved
I still have a job
still have someplace
to go
to escape you

but you're
on your fifth beer
and second blunt
and I can see
the mania
glassing over your eyes
and, oh how I wish
it was the weed
causing that shine
and the bass
from that
song I hate

that song by *Mary J Blige*
that you love
is on repeat
and I wonder how long
I can go on like this
before I'm hearing
voices
that aren't there
and seeing your
shadow men
and I know
even if you
pass out
there'll be no
sleep for me
because
every time
I close my eyes
I see your demons
shining back at me
and I realize

there's no
escaping you

Xtina Marie

delve
into my
depths
and swim
in the
abyss

Saturday Poets

fall..
slowly crashing
like
Saturday poets
awaiting
silence
with tears for
summer

Some Days

There are days
where nothing
goes as planned;
your favorite skirt
is stained,
traffic is brutal,
you burn the roast,
and *everyone* seems
moody…
all you really want
is some peace,
maybe a warm bath
or a tall glass
of white wine,
a few minutes
to scream
into your
pillow
and the arms
of the one
you love…

i can still
taste the
summer
on your lips
as you kiss me
with the sun
warming our
wind-blown skin

For the First Time

I heard your
voice
in my head
just like it
was yesterday
and I was
transported
back in time
to the
hours and hours
we spent
talking about
everything
and nothing
at the
same time,
when your voice
was the
last thing
I would hear
before falling
asleep
and it gave me
comfort
and
for the first time

I missed you

Never wander
beyond
the moon
where dreams
tempt

Healing Truths

lies
taught
ephemeral
love
so I
typed
healing
truths

Dry Ice

Dry ice
was my job
to acquire
for making
spooky fog
for the
Halloween party
we threw
every year
but all
I could think
about was
the beer you'd
drink
and the coke
you'd snort
before you'd
start in on me
and all of my
short comings
and how
you'd laugh
when I'd cry
and say

you were
just kidding
but we all
knew
you weren't
and the guests
would avert
their eyes,
embarrassed for me,
and wondering why
they'd agree
to come again
this year
when they all
knew
you'd never change

Blame
Willing
Wrongs

Mascara Tears

Mascara tears
slide soundlessly
down
my face
leaving
black stains
on porcelain
skin
as I cry out—
begging for
reprieve
respite
some mercy—
sweating
breathing harder
I suck in
gnash my teeth,
fingernails
digging fine lines
into the flesh
of my hands
I prepare
for the next blow
while you remind me

"stop" and "don't"
are not my
safe word

I meet
your gaze,
that gleam
in your eyes
the smile
on your lips
and I gasp out
"I know"

Something That Never Comes

It's only
in the dark
that she
comes for me
when the house
is quiet
and the
only sounds
I hear
are the
footsteps
down the
stairs,
the bare feet
padding
toward me
and I
pull the
sheet
higher
to cover
my head
as I wait
silently

for something
that
never
comes

Love
Took
Everything

Afternoon Kiss

an
afternoon
kiss
between
lovers
linger
in the
heart
like a
sigh

Willie Pearl

'Til we meet again, Nanny

If we all get
our own
personal heaven,
something
that's
just ours
alone,
I see
Willie Pearl
laughing
"Have mercy!"
and reminiscing
about the
good old days
while sipping on
an ice-cold Coors

Drunk

drunk on
whispers,
fingerprints
softly linger
like kisses
on delicate
flesh

All the Things

Life
gets in the
way,
gets too
loud,
allows
little annoyances
to permeate
fester
grow—
the kids
won't stop
arguing,
the dogs
won't stop
barking,
there are
never enough
hours in the
day
week
month
to accomplish
all the

things—
the things
we think are
important
but it's
not until
I'm lying
next to you—
can feel
the warmth
of your body—
at the end
of another
busy day
that
all the things
take a back seat

November

November
paints the
sky
with fire
that refuses
to warm,
sending
the dying
leaves
scattering
in vibrant red
and brilliant orange—
and the death
that surrounds
exhilarates

forgotten love
carries extinguished
sweetness
still desired

Faraway

honey,
music comes
from
faraway
dreamy
stories,
something
in-between
everything

Serenity

My serenity
is found
in the warmth
of your arms
as they
wrap
around me
at the end
of another
long day

Aphrodite

Let's make
magic
together
with just
the touch
of fingertips
dancing along
naked flesh
and watch
goosebumps
appear
as if
summoned
by the
goddess
of love,
herself

Quiet Love

home
the mountains
Paradise
a vision
of quiet love

Judgmental Bitch

sometimes
i hate
the woman
who stares
back at me
when I'm
striking
a pose
in the
mirror—
that
judgmental
bitch—
she never
has one
kind
word
to say to me
no matter
how hard
i try
for the
perfect
makeup

hairdo
outfit
and i can
never
find the right
angles
the right
lighting
to see the
beauty
others see
maybe...
just maybe
i need
to look
deeper

For Just One Day

There's this
magic
that happens
every
December—
this hush
in my soul
as I
countdown
to that
magical day
when all of the
day to day
worries and stresses
just…
stop
disappear
cease
and everything
is wonderful
blissful
otherworldly
even if
for

just one day

Xtina Marie

Perverse Hungers

The cool
 steel
of the
chains
weigh heavy
across
naked flesh,
a constant
reminder
that I
belong
to you,
that I'm
here
for
all of your
sadistic
needs
while you
feed
my
perverse
hungers

yesterday
describes
accurately
the sweet
symphony
memories
play across
flesh

Adore

I adore
the way the
light catches
your eyes
while they
watch me from
across the room
then crinkle
at the corners
when I catch you—
I adore the way
you adore me

Shallow Silhouette

For so
long
I played
the part—
the perfect
everything
to everyone,
no opinions
of my own,
no feelings
in which
to offend
anyone

and the
people
who didn't
know
me
were
complacent
with this
shallow
silhouette

of myself

but it's only
now
after I have
shed
that skin,
that I
finally
know
myself

Nectar

tease
nectar
with your
lips
as you
kiss
bare skin

Random Nonsense or Something Beautiful

sometimes I sit
and type
with no
sense
of where
it might go,
no definitive
story or idea
just
random
nonsense
that I hope
will turn into
something
beautiful
and oft times
I can't see
the masterpiece
I've created
through the
tears soaking
the keyboard
but just
because

I can't see it
doesn't mean
it's not there

Like Beasts

kissing
under the stars
like beasts—
long, deep
kisses
hungry for
the crash

Eggshells

I hated
living
your way,
always avoiding
the eggshells
you'd scattered
about
our lives,
the grenades
you'd toss
haphazardly
my way
when you were
feeling low,
too often
I'd cut my
feet
on the
shattered glass
strewn
around
carelessly,
left behind
after another

of your
drunken rages
or bipolar episodes—
yet even after
all of the
miles
I put
between us,
I still walk
softly
gingerly
cautiously,
and the hate
you cultivated
lives on

Enemies

Our country
stands
at this
crossroad;
two sides
so divided—
can they
ever
see eye
to eye
again?

can there
be a
truce,
are differences
of opinion
still allowed?

we await
hope
salvation
deliverance
from evils

either
real or imagined
and
pray
for better
days

will we
ever
realize
our
enemies
have never
been
each other?

dreams
of lovely
gardens
carry me
like flowers
hovering
with
the sun's
unearthly
beauty
in summer

Xtina Marie

Barefoot in the Moonlight

barefoot
in the
moonlight
my veins
howling
your name,
your heartbeat
my name

Xtina Marie

Together

everyday
together
we make
memories—
laughing
til our sides
ache,
heart to hearts
in bed
under
the covers,
hand in hand
strolling
outside
the plaza
on the
weekends,
reading silently
on the couch
in the evenings
while the chaos
of the kids
and the dogs
shatter the

stillness

together

Clarity

Too often
I get in
my own
way,
I overthink
way too
much,
I stress
about
the small
stuff…
I need some
escape,
a safe place
to hide,
retreat…
I find my
release
in the
bite
of the
crop
as it
dances

across
naked
vulnerable
flesh,
in the
thud
of the
flogger
as it
elicits
a scream
tearing
from
my raw
throat,
in the
crack
of the
paddle
as it
lights up
my ass
and sends
me
flying…
I find
clarity,
freedom

and it's
only then
that I
remember—
I'm
alive

And They Danced

And they
danced
to the song
that only they
could hear,
the music
softly
wafting
through
the air
around them,
the warm
glow
of the
moonlight
casting
shadows
on the walls,
and they
danced
through
the years
and the centuries
and the lives

that passed by
unnoticed,
the births
and deaths,
the birthdays,
the laughter
and all of
the tears,
and they
danced

Whiskey & Lies

He smelled
of whiskey
and lies
but I was
dehydrated
and dying of
thirst
and drank
them down
greedily
until
they were
running
over my
poisoned lips
and staining
the truths
I'd kissed
goodbye

Xtina Marie

Summer's Lovely Smile

laughter
and kisses
made
summer's
lovely smile
envious
of the
quiet
winter
darkness

it's early
the noise of
the city
softly
silent

Winter Constellations

poetic fingers
dance
under winter
constellations
while the
warmth
of the fire
remains

Junkie

We are all
addicts
underneath
the pretty
facade
of the adjusted,
kidding
ourselves
on just how
normal
society
tells us
we should be
while
searching
for the next
fix
of our
personal
shot of
whiskey
in whatever
form you
fancy...

some of us
just choose
to embrace that
addiction

Spent on Burning

spent
on burning,
nature
must know
darkness
just
in time
for the
future

Beyond

You take me
beyond—
every time
your hand heats
my ass
and you
order
me to
count
until
the numbers
start to blur
together
and time
stands still

Escaping You
part 2

The sound of your
voice
drowning
in the
alcohol
that courses
through
your already
toxic veins
snaps me
back in time
to a place
I swore
I'd left behind—
a place
I'd give anything
to never
ever
revisit…
that dark place
you forced me
to travel
with you

for longer
than I care
to admit,
memories
I wish
to bury
so far
beneath
the dirt
I no longer
smell
the death
that clings
to them,
that clings
to everything
you ever touched—
I let you
touch me
with those
skeletal fingers
that whispered
of dead and
decaying
things,
things that go
bump in
the night, things that

still
go bump in
the night,
that scatter like
cockroaches
or skittering
spiders
under the
harsh light
of a new
day
I've convinced
myself
I've escaped you
dawns
and
and
and
no matter
how long,
how hard
I try
there's
no
escaping
you

Demon Waltz

Your demons
waltz
freely
throughout
my head
whispering
nonsense
and other
gibberish
and I
follow
blindly
my hands
searching
for something
solid to
cling to
while I stumble
and grasp
onto the
nothing
surrounding
suffocating
oppressing me

silently
screaming
into the void
feeling my heart
rapidly pounding
my breaths
shallow and
catching
sweat breaking out
under my arms
and snaking
down my back
sending shivers
in its wake
and no matter
how many times
I exercise
expel
uninvite
these demons
I can't
shake them
because…

                        they are yours

So Close

i keep your
demons
at arms
length,
close enough
to feel
the warmth
of their
breath,
close enough
to allow
their
presence
to wreck
havoc
on my mind
so close
so close
so close
so close
so close
so close

Love is Loud

love is
loud—
it hurts
and burns
no matter
if you're
losing
or giving,
but it's still
the soul
by which we
artists
drink
our art

Love her like
you love
the Gods

Devotion

this
is what
devotion
looks like—
a delicate
caress
by strong
fingers,
adoration
evident
in his
gaze,
a whispered
I love you
in the dark;
warmth
on a cold
winter night,
and us

Silence the Screaming

Your
sickness
is infecting me,
a parasite
squirming
in the dark
matter
of my brain,
feeding off
whatever
nourishment
it can find,
escaping into
lonely corners
I've forgotten
exist,
whispering
to the
shadows
only we
can see
menacing
threats
and—

kill kill kill
I'm sorry,
did you say
something?
I could have
sworn—
disease ridden
thoughts—
What?
I can't hear
anything
through all
the screaming,
I wish
I could just
silence
the screaming
silence
the screaming
silence
the screaming

the screaming

the screaming

the screaming

the screaming

despite young
arrogant
dreams
or perhaps
maybe
because of,
I am content
with my
beautiful
forties

Wanderlust

the ache
behind
the routine
and wild
longing
for
adventure
in a
strange city
without
a map
screamed
in her soul
a song
of the
nomad,
the hippie,
the free spirit,
the wanderlust

Love Letters

Oft' times
I stare
at the sky
and wonder
if God
writes
love letters
to His
creations
in the clouds
and if we
just learned
His language
could we
decipher it?

Joannne
RIP 02/23/2021

She shed
that mortal
body,
the one
that failed
and mocked
her
for longer
than she
cared to
admit
remember
dwell on

on two feet
that could
once again
feel
the cool
tile
beneath them,
she whispered
a goodbye

to those
who'd loved
her,
and left
the pain
behind

Untold Secrets

the sky
remembers
untold secrets
we hold
within,
reminding us
in the breaths
dancing
on the wind

Not Aware

wary,
the silence is
uncertain
tentative
fearful
more dangerous

I retreat
to
my own
thoughts
quiet;
I keep my distance
not aware

Seasons

Is it just
the poets,
the empaths
and soul searchers
who feel
the electricity
humming
in the air
every time
the seasons
change
shift
renew,
when the
snow melts and
Mother Nature's
bite is a little
less sharp and
the sun slowly
becomes
less a liar
and more
a hope
for warmth,

Xtina Marie

when windows
open
to let the
smells
of spring
dance through
the house,
all fresh cut grass,
barbeques
and expectations—
when days
get longer
and we wait
for school
to end
and the sounds
of summer
to enchant
neighborhoods—
the children on bikes,
their laughter
infectious,
the dogs in a frenzy
barking at
every blade of grass
that dare move
and the feeling
of adventure

that skips
down the sidewalk,
praying
we make it last,
it makes
its mark
before
the chill
and the falling leaves
reminds us
that everything
eventually
ends

Xtina Marie

A Place I've Never Been

I'm called
to a place
I've never been
with tall
ceilings
and fancy
chandeliers,
drafty corridors
that hide
secrets
from centuries past
and long
moonless nights
with nothing
to do
but hold
your hand
and gaze into
the shadows—
I'm called
to a place
I've never been
but you're
always

by my side

Thrill Me

delightfully
electric
currents
tighten
my belly
when you
thrill me
with lips
softly wet
from silky
loving,
tongue
pressed
taut
against
damp
sensations

Pages to Go

I often
fantasize
about life—
lazy and quiet—
the two of us
lounging in bed
til noon
on a Saturday
bare skin
warm from
the blankets
tangled around
and under us,
perhaps sipping
something warm
on a cold day
or reading
leisurely
with no thought
to chores
and work
and kids
—the daily grind—
and then

I hear
the laughter
waft in
from the
living room,
the dogs
barking,
and I'm
content
that for now,
this chapter
still has
pages to go

I'm Sorry

I'm sorry—
not because
we fell apart
or that I
couldn't
love you
the way you
needed
or that
you demanded
way more
than you
ever gave
or that I lived
in fear
of something
that probably
never really came,
at least not
in any real
sense—
no, you never
hit me,
but your

words
hurt more
than that
black eye
I got
in the 4th grade
when Tommy
threw that
dodge ball
directly at me
on purpose,
I might add—
and sometimes
in a rather
unpleasant fight
I'd scream out
and dare you
to hit me
because
this pain…
this pain
was one
of those
deep pains
that cause
eternal
damage,
the kind

not seen by
the naked eye
but never quite
goes away
and all of
the sorrys
all together
in the history
of sorrys
doesn't make
a lick of difference
because
you'll never
forgive me
for not wanting
to take
your abuse
any longer

Summer Freedoms

eating strawberries
in the afternoons
as we sit
under the
sun's warmth,
feet bare
and unfazed
in the countryside,
my soul sighs
at the blossoming
summer freedom

just remember…
consequence
has griefs
unknown
and
unsought

Xtina Marie

Change

Some people say
I've changed—
but I've just
put to bed
some demons,
water under the bridge,
said goodbye to yesterdays
and a handful of
other cliches
we grow so tired of
yet spew out like
warm soda—
flat and tasteless,
and so very
undesirable

And maybe
I *have* changed

Smiles
come easier,
the darkness
doesn't seem quite
so *dark* now

and I've
stopped
being scared
of my own shadow

Ravenous

The marks
he leaves
behind
are little
tell-tale
signs
that he's
ravenous
for the
taste
of me
fresh from
sleep,
hair mussed,
skin warm
from his bed
and his guttural
growls
rumbling
in my ear
ignite
my hunger

hems of
floral skirts
get shorter
as the bright
warm touch
of spring
teases

Something Cheerful

Spring has sprung—
the windchimes
are playing
my favorite tune,
something cheerful
that only
the birds
know the words to
while the sun
darts from behind
the million clouds
teasing my skin
and warming
the grass
tickling
my bare feet

Everything Will Burn

Dressed
in red
she tore
through
the streets;
alarming
violent

*everything
will burn!*

Something Chocolate

The receipt
was old
and crumpled,
faded some
in certain spots
but I could still
make out the
3 Musketeers
candy bar
toward the bottom
and I spiraled
back to
then
and standing
in the door
of your room
annoyed
and asking
what you wanted
from the store
something chocolate
and so
I didn't even
bother

to write that down—
I'd remember it…
and I did,
but not until
I was already
in the checkout line
and I remember
annoyance again
flashed through me
as I searched for
that damned
candy bar
something chocolate
and now
how I wish
you were still here,
still annoying me
and asking me
to get you
something chocolate
but you're not
and I can't
look at a
3 Musketeers
without
thinking of your
something chocolate

I Know Nothing

There was a time
when I knew
your every move…
when, at any
given time
I would have known
what you were doing,
the number of
coffee cups
you were on,
what you were
watching
on television
or what book
lay open
on your nightstand—
when I could
set my watch
to the time
you'd go out
for the last
cigarette
of the night
or know when

you'd need to
run to the store
because you were
getting low
on coke
for your whiskey…
and sometimes
when it's quiet
I can still
hear the sound
of your screen door
squeaking shut
or your zippo
sliding against
the pantleg
of your jeans
and I start to smile
before remembering
there was a time
I knew
everything
but now
now
I know
nothing

Forever Frozen

The old photo album
was yellowed with age,
in fact, I'd never
seen it any other way,
although I suspect
it had been a
creamy white
once upon a time…
the pages were
soft from wear
and a slight mildewy—
although not terribly
unpleasant—
smell seeped out
with every turn…
hours were spent
as a child
holding the album
across knobby knees,
usually scabbed over
from a spill while
racing up and down
the asphalt
in my roller skates—

the white ones
with the hot pink
stopper at the toe...
candid smiles
forever frozen
as shadows from the past
pose for the camera,
hamming it up...
my grandma
as a young woman,
on the arm of
my grandfather—
boy did he have style!
in his purple pastel suit
with matching tie,
a drink in hand;
champagne? Fine wine?
perhaps just a beer,
I'll never know...
my mother
holding an infant,
and I can still see
that scar on her arm,
the one I was convinced
was a milk stain
for too many
embarrassing years...
anniversary parties

and birthdays
and holidays
and some pictures
clearly for no other reason
but to immortalize
the moment,
and not once
in all of those hours
spent turning the pages
did I ever think to
thank the inventor of
photography…

but now,
older, some wrinkles
lining eyes needing glasses
to better see the pages

I am grateful

About the Author

The Short Version:
Book Publisher, Poet, Podcaster, Writer,
Mom, Bibliophile…

The Accidental Poet:

Xtina Marie is an avid horror and fiction genre reader, who became a blogger; who became a published poet; who became an editor; who now is a book publisher and CEO of Hell Bound Books Publishing with her co-host on The Panic Room Radio Show, James H. Longmore.

Her first book of poetry, Dark Musings has received outstanding reviews. It is likely Xtina was born to this calling. Writing elaborate twisted tales to entertain her classmates in middle school would later lead Xtina to use her poetry as a private emotional outlet in adult life—words she was hesitant to share publicly—but the more she shared, the more accolades her writing received.

She has two additional poetic narrative editions, Light Musings and Darkest Sunlight, a combination of both light and dark poetry. In 2018, Xtina fell in love with free verse, and began writing Without the Confines of My Rhymes, which was released in 2019. In 2020 she released her follow up free verse book, Immortalize Me.

Xtina has contributed works to the following:
Suite 269 by Christine Zolendz
Busted Lip: An Anthology
Monsters of Metal: An Anthology
The Intermission, Gore Carnival Book 2
A Lovely Darkness: Poetry with Heart
Black Candy: A Halloween Anthology of Horror
Collected Christmas Horror Shorts by Kevin J. Kennedy
Slashing Through the Snow: A Christmas Horror Anthology
Depraved Desires: Volume 1
Beautiful Tragedies
Damsels of Distress
Pieces of Us: A Collection of Flash Fiction, Short Stories, and Poetry
Subliminal Messages: A Collection of Poetry, Prose, and Quotes
Leaves of the Poet Tree by Andrew Aitken
Apocalypse of the Heart by Leah Negron and friends

Poetry Friends in Rhythm & Rhyme by Leah Negron
Graveyard Girls by Gerri R. Gray
Further Within Darkness & Light: A Collection of
Poetry by Paul B Morris
The Light Shines Through: Anthology of Poetry
Paper Cuts
Other titles by Xtina:
Light Musings
Darkest Sunlight
Without the Confines of My Rhymes
Immortalize Me

Xtina resides in the beautiful state of Tennessee, with
her family and three yapping ankle biters.

You can find Xtina:
http://www.hellboundbookspublishing.com/index.html
https://www.facebook.com/XtinaMarie4031/
https://www.facebook.com/ThePanicRoomRadioShow/
https://www.amazon.com/Xtina-
Marie/e/B01E1QNI3O?ref=sr_ntt_srch_lnk_1&qid=158
9142288&sr=8-1

OTHER POETRY FROM HELLBOUND BOOKS
www.hellboundbookspublishing.com

Immortalize Me

"Immortalize Me is raw, beautiful, and poignant. This subtle yet hypnotic dance between darkness and light is a poetry lover's delight!"
- USA Today Bestselling Author, K Webster

With a style echoing the late Audre Lorde, Xtina Marie's newest poetry collection Immortalize Me - with its striking imagery and layered free-verse simplicity - reveals a provocative, candid look at Xtina's story told in fragments - intimate snapshots of moments of submission and raw passion, nostalgia and drifting daydreams, anguish and quiet contemplation. All in all, a bold, haunting, bittersweet collection.

"As lyrical as song and as faceted as a diamond, Xtina Marie's latest collection is a riot of imagery and emotion that pushes buttons and boundaries alike. IMMORTALIZE ME does just what it says - her words will linger in your blood long after the last page has been read."
- Alistair Cross, author of The Book of Strange Persuasions and the Vampires of Crimson Cove series

"Xtina Marie's words punch you in the gut, hit you in the feels, and put you in her past in a way that forces you to confront your own. She wields a pen the way witches wave wands... purely magic."
- Carver Pike (horror and dark fantasy author)

Without the Confines of my Rhymes

Poetry is a beautiful thing, illustrating thoughts and emotions with concise, well-chosen words. A lot of poetry rhymes, adding additional flavor to the words, giving them a sense of rhythm, of flow

But what happens when you take away the rhyming, when you cast off the forms of convention and good sense?

Then the interesting things begin to come out. When the next line doesn't need to rhyme, anything can come next. As it is within the poems themselves, so it is with this book in its entirety.

Casting off the rhyming styles she used before, Xtina Marie embarks on a journey of emotional ups and downs, reflecting on love, loss, children and art.

So settle in, put on your wine-colored glasses, and take a trip without the confines of rhymes.

Darkest Sunlight

"The heart was made to be broken." - *Oscar Wilde*

To allow your heart to soar, you must risk the depths. Darkest Sunlight is the third poetic narrative from Xtina Marie. In this journey, readers will begin in the darkest of places yet revealed to us by this critically acclaimed poet, only to then find themselves thrust into the brightness of love before their eyes and minds can fully adjust. It is this shocking contrast which best conveys what it is to love, lose, and love again.

In Dark Musings, Xtina explored sadness. In Light Musings, she explored the intricacies of a loving heart. In Darkest Sunlight, Xtina Marie compares the opposite ends of the spectrum, and in doing so, she found a place darker than black.

Dark Musings

The perfect companion piece to Light Musings – The dark side of Xtina Marie's poetry delves into intense emotions: heartache, loss, hurt, pain, rage, and a dangerous consuming love which can drive one insane. Dark Musings is not a collection!

The author returned to the centuries old practice of Narrative Poetry—the telling of a story through poetry. If you believe you are brave enough to explore the savage emotions of the human heart; Dark Musings will test your mettle.

Light Musings

The perfect companion piece to Dark Musings – an intriguing mirror image of the darkness you have just read, but no less deep and soul stirring.

What a web she weaves. Light Musings is a poetic narrative—a story told through related poems. Xtina Marie is a master of this style. Known by her fans as the Dark Poet Princess, this term of endearment came about as a result of the horror genre embracing her first book: Dark Musings which continues to garner stellar reviews. Light Musings will not disappoint her loyal fans as darkness is present within these pages as well. However, this latest book will show a much larger audience that Xtina's poetry pulls out every feeling the reader has ever experienced—forcing them to feel with her protagonist. Light Musings shows us that love is made from darkness and light; something Xtina Marie explores like no one else.

Gray Skies of Dismal Dreams

Prepare for an excursion into a gloomy world of shadows, where the days are never sunlit and blithe, and where the nights are wrapped in endless nightmares.

No happy endings or silver linings are found in the clouds that fill these gray skies.

But what you will find, gathered in one volume, are the darkest of poems and tales of horror, waiting to take your mind on a journey into realms of the uncheerful and the unholy.

An amazingly surreal collection of short stories and the darkest of poetry, all interspersed with stunning graveyard photographs taken by the multitalented author herself - an absolute must for every bookshelf!

Beautiful Tragedies

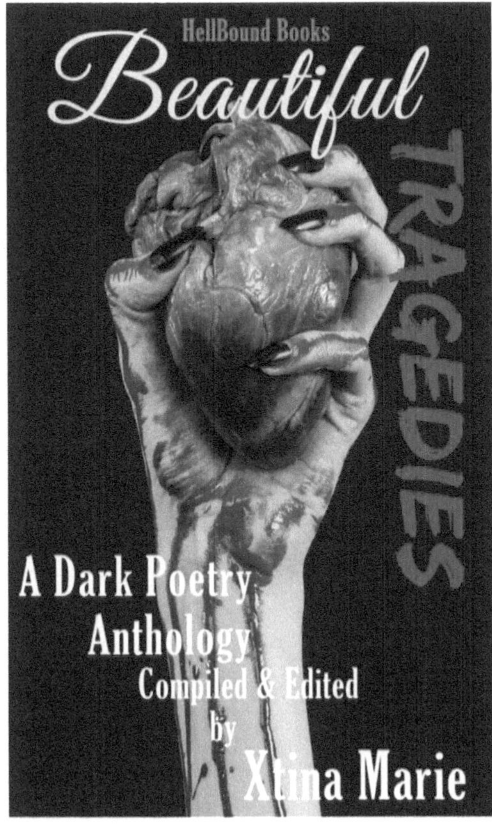

Only through dark poetry can a tragedy become something truly beautiful.

"Beauty is in the eye of the beholder." This phrase has origins dating back to ancient Greece, circa 300 BC; proving that some humans have always had the ability to see beauty where others could not.

Beautiful Tragedies is a compilation of 140 works by no less than fifty-five amazing poets writing in a variety of forms--all inspired by feelings born in the darkest of times.

Xtina Marie

**A HellBound Books LLC
Publication**

www.hellboundbookspublishing.com

Printed in the United States of America